Anyhow, I'm Glad I Tried
Story and Pictures by
Judith Vigna
ALBERT WHITMAN & Company, Chicago

Published simultaneously in Canada by
General Publishing, Limited, Toronto.
Printed in the United States of America.
Second Printing 1980

Library of Congress Cataloging in Publication Data

Vigna, Judith.
Anyhow, I'm glad I tried.

SUMMARY: A child treats a disagreeable classmate with kindness and is glad she makes an attempt at friendliness even though she feels her effort is in vain.

(1. Kindness—Fiction) I. Title
PZ7.V67An (E) 78-12883
ISBN 0-8075-0378-9

Irma Jane is the meanest person
in my whole class.

She says bad things about me
behind my back.

She puts up
her pictures
on top of mine—

IRMA
JANE
ME

—and pokes things into me
when I take a test.

Irma Jane is so mean,

I wish she'd get lost

and never be found, ever.

Mother says
I should try to be nice
to her.
She says Irma Jane
is unhappy because
she has no friends,
and her grandmother
makes her wear
funny clothes.

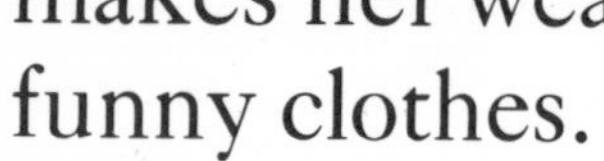

But when I'm nice
and share my brownies
she throws my lunch box
in the wastebasket.

I really despise Irma Jane.

Today is Irma Jane's birthday.
I'd like to give her a big
spiky lollipop and make
her teeth fall out.

But I'm going to try
to be nice to her.
Just for her birthday.

"Happy birthday, Irma Jane," I say.

"Beat it," she says.

"I hope you drown in boiling spaghetti!"
I say to myself.

Then I remember and call—

"Wait, Irma Jane—
I have something for you."

"My mother baked you a cake
for your birthday.

It's only a little one,
but it's just for you."

"Hmm. I'll bet it's full of bugs and worms.

I'll bet it's poisoned,

and you’ll dance on my grave!”

I'm never going to be nice to her again.

NEVER, NEVER, NEVER.

happy birthday
to
me!

I guess I'll never know
if she liked her cake.

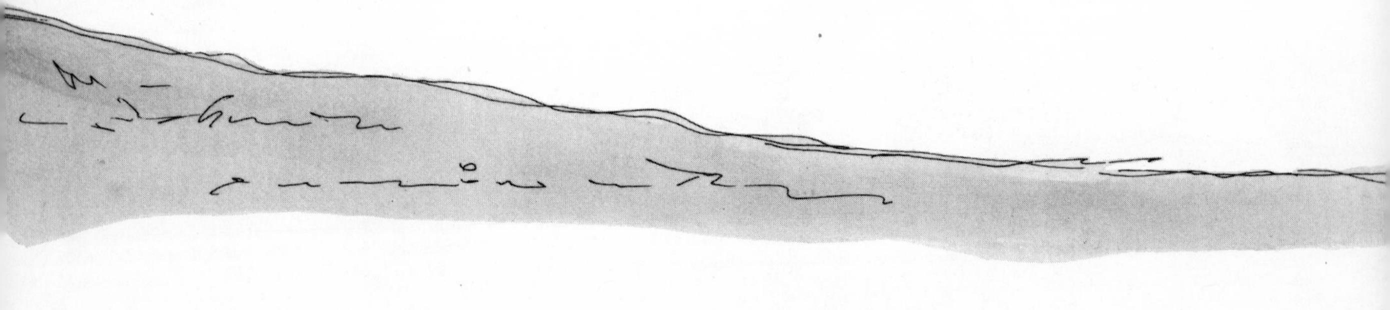

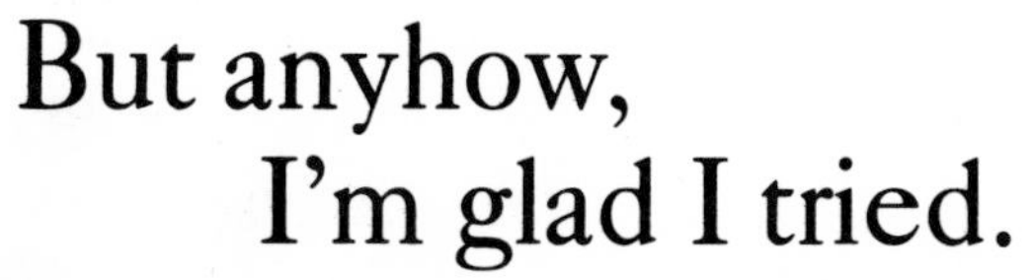

But anyhow,
I'm glad I tried.

MANAGEMENT SYSTEMS CORPORATION, CIRCA
3 3985 60003 3867